# Also by John Sager

# CONQUERING
# COVID

# JOHN SAGER

InspiringVoices®

Inspiring Voices books may be ordered through booksellers or by contacting:

Inspiring Voices
1663 Liberty Drive
Bloomington, IN 47403
www.inspiringvoices.com
1 (866) 697-5313

Because of the dynamic nature of the Internet, any web addresses or links contained in this book may have changed since publication and may no longer be valid. The views expressed in this work are solely those of the author and do not necessarily reflect the views of the publisher, and the publisher hereby disclaims any responsibility for them.

Any people depicted in stock imagery provided by Getty Images are models, and such images are being used for illustrative purposes only. Certain stock imagery © Getty Images.

ISBN: 978-1-4624-1303-4 (sc)
ISBN: 978-1-4624-1304-1 (e)

Library of Congress Control Number: 2020911353

Print information available on the last page.

Inspiring Voices rev. date: 08/15/2020

# ACKNOWLEDGEMENT

As with many of my writings, I want to thank my long-time friend and fellow fly fisherman Sanford Young. Stan and I both are in our nineties and no longer able to fish, but we do have fond memories of the good old days when we were able to fish together. Stan has perused every line of this work and where they are any glitches, typos or other mistakes, they are mine, not his. Thank you, Stan!

# AUTHOR'S COMMENT

Although this is a novel—the story traces the development of the novel Coronavirus from its origins to Wuhan, China to its present status as a world-wide pandemic—I use a number of online resources to provide known facts when these are appropriate.

One of these follows, from an unknown author but one who speaks with knowledge and authority.

*   *   *

Feeling confused as to why Coronavirus is a bigger deal than seasonal flu? Here it is in a nutshell. It has to do with RNA sequencing, that is, *genetics.*

Seasonal flu is an "all human virus". The DNA/RNA chains that make up the virus are recognized by the human immune system. This means that your body has some immunity to it before it comes around each year... you get immunity two ways...through exposure to a virus, or by getting a flu shot.

Novel viruses come from animals.... the World Health Organization tracks novel viruses in animals, (sometimes for years watching for mutations). Usually these viruses only transfer from animal to animal (pigs in the case of H1N1) (birds in the case of the Spanish flu). But as soon as one of these animal viruses mutates, and starts to transfer from animals to humans, then it's a problem, Why? Because humans have no natural or acquired immunity; the RNA sequencing of the genes inside the virus isn't human, and the human immune system doesn't recognize it so we can't fight it off.

Now, sometimes, the mutation only allows transfer from animal to human, for years its only transmission is from an infected animal to a human before it finally mutates so that it can now transfer from human to human. When that happens we have a new contagion phase. And depending on the fashion of this new mutation, that's what decides how contagious, or how deadly it's going to be.

H1N1 was deadly, but it did not mutate in a way that was as deadly as the Spanish flu. Its RNA was slower to mutate and it attacked its host differently, too.

Fast forward.

Now, here comes this Coronavirus; it existed in animals only, for nobody knows how long; but one day, at an animal market in Wuhan China, in December 2019, it mutated and made the jump from animal to people. At first, only animals could give it to a person. But, here's the scary part: in just TWO WEEKS it mutated again and gained the ability to jump from human to human. Scientists call this quick ability, "slippery."

This Coronavirus, not being in any form a "human" virus (whereas we would all have some natural or acquired immunity), took off like a rocket. And this was because humans have no known immunity; doctors have no known medicines for it.

And it just so happens that this particular mutated animal virus changed itself in such a way that it causes great damage to human lungs.

That's why Coronavirus is different from seasonal flu, or H1N1 or any other type of influenza. And it's a lung-eater.

For this one, we really have no tools in our shed History has shown that fast and immediate closings of public places has helped in the past pandemics. Philadelphia and Baltimore were reluctant to close events in 1918 and they were the hardest hit in the US during the Spanish Flu epidemic.

Factoid: Henry VIII stayed in his room and allowed no one near him, till the Black Plague passed. Just like us, he had no tools in his shed, except social isolation.

And let me end by saying that right now it's hitting older folks harder; but this genome is so slippery that if it mutates again—and it will— who's to say, what it will do next?

# ONE

January 1, 2020.

Zhang Wei Ying awoke to the buzzing of his iPhone. He recognized the voice; it was his cousin Li Wei, calling from his apartment in Wuhan. But before he could speak, the signal faded, then went silent.

"That's okay. I can call him back after I've finished breakfast. Curious, though, that his call didn't come through. It's probably something to do with the government's attempt to monitor calls coming from Wuhan, what with all the trouble they're having there. Last I heard, fifty or so of the residents in his building were seriously ill and trying to get medical help, some kind of bad virus, apparently."

**\* \* \***

Years earlier, when Zhang Wei was in his teens, his parents determined that their eldest child would make something of himself. For Mr. and Mrs. Ying it had been a difficult time. His only work was tending the rice paddies, some 15 kilometers from their home and 400 kilometers from the center of Beijing . In their village, owning an automobile was something only the local Communist village commandant—the much despised and feared Ye Ru Yong—could afford. Most folks either walked or rode bicycles and that is how Zhang Wei's father went to and from his work. When the family was at home, they never spoke of their awful living conditions. Why should they? The neighbors next door were no better off. And there was always the possibility that whatever they said would be overheard and then reported to Ye Ru. He was known to attend Communist Party cell meetings, first Monday of every month, seven o'clock sharp. It was assumed that at these meetings, Ye Ru's comrades would share whatever tid-bits had been gathered and report them to higher authority.

It was this neighbor snitching on neighbor syndrome that persuaded the Ying family never to join the Communist Party. This, despite that fact that everyone knew that if one wanted to succeed, party membership was required.

* * *

In his school years, Zhang Wei's friends knew that he came from a family that abhorred the country's Communist leadership. A few of his closest friends came from families who felt the same way and theirs was a coveted friendship.

When it came time for Zhang Wei to apply for admission to Beijing University's School of Medicine, he deliberately falsified his paperwork, claiming to come from a family dedicated to the Communist cause in which both parents were party members. He knew he was chancing being found a liar, but he thought that just maybe the investigators would fail to notice.
And fail they did.

* * *

Four and a half years later, Zhang Wei had finished his course work, endured six hours of oral examinations, then the written tests which consumed parts of four days. Finally, he was handed his diploma by the university's Commissar of Medicine. His mother and father had long since passed away and his brother had found work in far-off Shanghai and was unable to attend. But, henceforth, if he wished, he could be addressed as *Doctor* Zhang Wei Ying.

* * *

He had an important appointment to keep and it was important that it be successful. His search had led him to an official at the American embassy, a man he had heard about some months earlier.

Terry Bradford had established something of a reputation for himself. He brought with him to his post, his wife, a Chinese-American woman, a Christian, who had already begun a kindergarten class in the embassy building's basement. In the class were ten children, five Americans and five Chinese whose parents worked for the embassy as local employees. The woman was teaching the Chinese children to speak English and the American children to speak Mandarin. It was a newsworthy event, duly reported in most Chinese newspapers and on several television channels.

But why Bradford? Because he was the head of the embassy's consular office, one of whose functions was to issue visitor's visas to Chinese applicants.

In Bradford's office:

"Mr. Ying, I see that you've completed the necessary forms and that your wife is expecting you to join her within the next sixty days."

"That's right. Shortly after we were married she got word that her cousin was very ill and not expected to live. So she got a visitor's visa, flew to San Francisco and was able to be with her cousin for the last ten days of her life.

Now, she lives in San Francisco's Chinese-American community and works as a nurse in a Christian hospital. She's a valuable asset because her English is almost as good as her Mandarin."

"I don't have problem with granting your request for a visa. But before I do that I have a question or two."

"Sure, go ahead."

"You say you have a cousin who lives in Wuhan?"

"Yes, his name is Li Wei. He lives in an apartment complex on Zhing Ho Avenue, along with about fifty others."

"And have you heard from him recently?"

"Yes, early this morning - - - well, sort of. He called me on his cell but the signal dropped out before he could finish. I assumed it had to with the government's attempt to monitor calls from Wuhan, what with all the sick people who live there. I assume our leaders in Beijing are trying to keep this from leaking to the West."

"Mr. Ying, it should come as no surprise to you to learn—if you don't know it already—that we Americans have a consulate in Wuhan. It's one of your country's principal transportation hubs, located as it is astride the Yangtze River and several foreign tour companies have facilities there including the popular Viking River Cruises. With a population of more than eleven million people it's a city in which we Americans want to be represented."

"Okay, I understand that. What else do I need to know?"

"Those sick people you mentioned. We know how they got sick.""

"You *do*?"

"Yes. Wuhan has several animal markets. Many Chinese people enjoy shopping at these markets where they can purchase things like cooked squid, frozen crab legs, pickled locusts, even pieces of broiled snake.

"Every now and then, we've learned, these animal parts have been infected with a virus, that virus—very recently—has been given a name: the novel Coronavirus. And that virus is able to transfer itself to those unfortunate souls who eat that kind of food.

"That is why those sick people you mentioned have fallen ill. And, worse, every sick person can pass the virus—by coughing or sneezing—to anyone who is within a few meters. In other words, it's an exponential explosion that Wuhan is dealing with.

"You mentioned a fading voice signal on your iPhone."

"Yes, I did."

"We now believe that is part of your government's attempt to prevent the world from learning the truth about what is happening in Wuhan. We Americans would call this a massive coverup. But it will be impossible for that coverup to succeed. There may be as many as several hundred cases of Covid 19—the name now given to the Coronavirus-induced illness—in Wuhan. These people talk to each other. The city's hospitals already are overwhelmed with sick people seeking treatment.

"I would advise you not to return to Wuhan. Find passage from Beijing to San Francisco as soon as possible. In another week or so, finding passage on *any* carrier may be impossible.

"And, I wish you well."

# TWO

*Thursday, January 23, 2020, in the office of James Thurston, the Wall Street Journal's overseas news editor. He's speaking to one of his assistants, Toby Axelrod.*

"Toby, our boss wants us to provide more coverage of this Coronavirus story. For example, we haven't heard from our man in Beijing, Don Whitehead. That's because he's been covering the latest Communist Party plenum meeting but he should drop that and provide more copy on what's going down in Wuhan. Would you please send him an email and ask him to do that? Tell him he's authorized to fly to Wuhan and find a hotel that's still open to foreign journalists, preferable one that shows no signs of being infected by this damned virus!"

"Sure thing, Jim. I'll get right on it."

*   *   *

*One week later this article appeared in the Journal's* Foreign News *section.*

# MASSIVE COVERUP IN CHINA

By Donald Whitehead.
Wuhan, Hubei Province, the Peoples' Republic of China

I soon learned that there's only one hotel in this nearly locked-down city that accepts bookings for foreign journalists. Using my best Mandarin, I persuaded the hotel's manager to give me a room at the usual rate,1000 yuan. (That's about $175 American.) The room comes with breakfast and one of their morning newspapers, which I ignore, preferring to watch television.

The tricky part of this assignment has been finding those few residents of Wuhan who are willing to talk about what *really* happened here, during those awful days when Covid 19 began taking its deadly toll. I've used a digital voice recorder to capture those interviews in which the man or woman understood who I am and why I'm doing this. In other instances, I've spoken with a few medical professionals, those who know their stories are likely to go viral once printed. That said, I'll try to summarize.

* * *

While Chinese authorities continued to insist that the virus could not spread from one person to another, some doctors aren't so sure. One doctor warned that Wuhan should implement the strictest possible monitoring system for a new viral pneumonia that has infected hundreds of people, and that almost certainly it is being transmitted from one person to another.

Another questionable statement: The Wuhan Municipal Health Commission published this: "Preliminary investigations have shown no clear evidence of human-to-human transmission and no medical staff infections."

A few days later, Chinese medical authorities claimed to have identified the virus and asserted that there is no evidence that the virus is readily spread by humans, which would make it particularly dangerous. Nor has not been linked to any deaths.

More from the Wuhan Municipal Health Commission. "All 739 close contacts, including 419 medical staff, have undergone medical observation and no related cases have been found. Further, no evidence of human-to-human transfer has been found.

Another curiosity: Political leaders in Hubei Province, which includes Wuhan, began their regional meeting. In the course of four days, the Coronavirus was never mentioned.

Despite the fact that Wuhan doctors know the virus is contagious, city authorities allowed some 40 thousand families to gather and share home-cooked food at a Lunar New Year banquet.

By now, my sources tell me, millions of people have left Wuhan, carrying the virus all over China and into other countries.

*   *   *

The story of the Coronavirus is still being written. But at this early date we can see all kinds of moments where different decisions could have lessened the severity of the outbreak. Readers probably have heard variations of: 'Chinese authorities denied that the virus could be transferred from human to human, until it was too late.' What readers probably have not heard is how emphatically, loudly and repeatedly the Chinese government insisted human transmission is impossible, long after doctors in Wuhan had concluded human transmission was ongoing—and how the World Health Organization assented to that conclusion, despite the suspicions of other outside health experts.

Clearly, the US government's response to this threat was not nearly robust enough, and not enacted anywhere near quickly enough. Most

European governments weren't prepared, either. Few governments around the world were or are prepared for the scale of the danger. We can only wonder whether accurate information from China would have altered the way the US government, the American people, and the world prepared for the oncoming danger of infection.

*  *  *

That's enough for one day. I'm going back to my hotel room, take a shower and try to get a good night's sleep. If my editor approves, I'll be on the next plane back to Beijing. But, as the virus is now all over China, I may have to return to New York. That would be just fine. I haven't seen my wife and kids for more than a year.

# THREE

Zhang Wei was lucky. The rulers in Beijing had not yet imposed air travel restrictions on its population, only surface transportation where person-to-person contact was more likely to spread the virus. He caught a commuter flight from Beijing to Shanghai, then found that his reservation on China Eastern Airlines was still in order, non-stop Shanghai to San Francisco. Although he could have afforded business or even first class, he chose to fly coach, assuming he would be able to talk to the average Chinese citizen, not an official or military officer who could afford the higher fares.

His travel agent had told him that China Eastern posted its fares in both dollars and yuan, the dollar the more stable of the two. Zhang Wei's one-way ticket—on an Air Bus A320—cost him slightly less that 4,000 yuan, or the equivalent of $541.00.

Within moments of finding his assigned seat, he realized the coach section was nearly empty, only ten other passengers scattered throughout the huge cabin and in first and business class not a single seat was occupied. As the flight attendant explained over the intercom, every passenger was expected to don a mask, to be found in the nearest seat pocket. The captain had strict instructions not to leave his assigned gate until this requirement had been met.

* * *

After reaching cruising altitude the seat belt sign turned off and the few passengers were free to move about the cabin, but only if they continued to wear a mask. One of the flight attendants sat down beside Zhang Wei and asked him if he was feeling okay.

"Sure, why do you ask?"

"We're required to do that. Some of our passengers suffer from air sickness but, even more important, the regs require us to be sure no one aboard has been infected. I have one of those no-touch thermometers and I'm going to hold it about a centimeter from your forehead. Okay? - - - Good, you're normal, so not to worry."

"How can your airline make any money with so few passengers?"

"That's a good question and the answer lies in Beijing. Our rulers really don't care, so long as we keep flying. It's a prestige thing. Frankly, I think they're a bunch of idiots—and I wouldn't say that except that you hold a one-way ticket and I presume you won't be coming back."

"True. My wife lives in San Francisco and I'll be living with her. I understand the American government will issue what they call a resident alien permit and if the foreigner doesn't mess up, he/she can apply for a Green Card; and that, as you probably know, leads to American citizenship.

"You married?"

"Not yet. And what business is that of yours!?"

"Hey, easy! You're attractive, probably not yet thirty. You probably have a boyfriend, somewhere."

"I do. And we plan to marry as soon as this crazy virus problem is fixed. Our wise men in Beijing say it should be all okay within the year. I think they're lying. They must think we're all a bunch of fools, to believe that."

"Well, it's been good talking to you. You stay well, promise?

"I'll try."

**\*   \*   \***

"Not bad," he said to himself. "I wish there were more like her, people who aren't afraid to kick back against those know-nothings in Beijing. But while I'm at it, there's a guy sitting a few rows ahead and he may be willing to chat."

The 'guy a few rows ahead' turned out to be Dr. Christopher Lee, a Chinese-American physician, now returning to America from a one-year internship program at Beijing's United Family Health & Wellness Center. Dr. Lee reluctantly agreed to allow Zhang Wei to sit beside him, aware of the new 'social distance' rules as promulgated by the CDC in Atlanta, Georgia.

**\*   \*   \***

"You speak English?"

"I do. And you?"

"Okay, have a seat but keep that face mask in place. It's one of my rules, the newest one."

"Thanks. I'm Zhang Wei Ying, but you can call me Zhang Wei."

"Hmm, I detect a slight Mandarin accent, would that be right?"

"That's my native tongue, how did you guess?"

"I didn't guess. It's obvious."

"And you?"

"I'm doctor Gerald Lee. I'm an American physician, born of Chinese-American parents 45 years ago in San Francisco. So, yes, I speak both English and Mandarin. It's been part of my job for the past year."

"How's that?"

"Yes. I've been serving a one-year internship program at Beijing's United Family Health & Wellness Center. I've treated, maybe, a hundred patients, some in the emergency ward, a few in the ICU but most in normal recovery circumstances.

"But all that changed a few weeks ago when people started showing up with this novel Coronavirus infection. Within ten days, the hospital had run out of beds, as many as ten or so staff had become infected, so they're too sick to work. The hospital's chief administrator begged the Ministry of Health to provide enough information to tell us what we were dealing with. They said it was 'a temporary aberration' that should disappear within two weeks. Of course, now I understand this was part of the government's attempt to prevent the outside world from knowing what was really happening.

"When I get back to my practice in Tulsa, I'm going to write a detailed report about what I've learned and I'll send it to the CDC in Atlanta. As soon as the American medical profession learns about this, things will have to change."

# FOUR

As soon as Zhang Wei had worked his way though the San Francisco airport's immigration and customs windows, he found his way baggage claim carousel No. 2. As he had hoped, his wife, Yu Yan, was standing there, waiting for him. After a fierce embrace:

"My God, Sweetheart, it's so good to see you! We thought you'd never be able to leave, what with all the restrictions we've heard about."

"Actually, Yu Yan, it wasn't all that difficult. I've kept my opinions to myself and the authorities had no reason to be suspicious. The American officials could not have been more helpful. So, here I am!"

"Good. I've hired a porter and he'll take your luggage to my car. We can use the electric train to get to the parking lot."

"What kind of car?"

"It's a Mercedes SL 360 convertible, one year old. Unfortunately, it rains in these parts as much as it doesn't, but on nice days it's fun to drive with the top down."

"How can you afford that? You robbed a bank?"

"No, Silly, of course not. I'm paying for it one month at a time. As you'll soon learn, I'm something of mover and shaker—as we say when we're speaking English—in my community. In case you haven't heard, it's known as Chinatown, one of San Francisco's major tourist attractions. Here's a brochure you can read on our way to the parking lot."

* * *

*San Francisco's Chinatown is the oldest of its kind in North America and the largest Chinese enclave outside Asia. Since its establishment in 1848, it has been highly important and influential in the history and culture of ethnic Chinese immigrants in North America. The community continues to retain its own customs, languages, places of worship, social clubs and identity.. There are two hospitals, several parks and squares, numerous churches, a post office, and other infrastructure. Recent immigrants, many of whom are elderly, opt to live in Chinatown because of the availability of affordable housing and their familiarity with the culture. San Francisco's Chinatown is also renowned as a major tourist attraction, drawing more visitors than the Golden Gate Bridge.*

* * *

"Finished? Now then, Dearest., the brochure you just read mentions two hospitals. I work in one of those, St. Mary's Mercy Hospital. Years ago I got my license as an RN, that means Registered Nurse. St. Mary's is supported by the city's Catholic Archdiocese, led by Bishop Jonathan Wagner. He's in his eighties now and is talking about retirement. The good bishop has maintained a hands-off attitude when it comes to the hospital's management. That would be fine in normal times but these times aren't normal - - -"

"The Coronavirus?"

"Exactly that. The hospital has something like 400 beds, and all but eighty or so are occupied by patients suffering from Covid 19. Every day, at least four or five of these patients dies because we don't have any way of keeping them alive. And we won't until somebody develops a vaccine that works. There's a hearse on duty 24/7 and it is continually moving back and forth from the hospital to one of the city's morgues. The morgue managers tells us they're about to run out of space. So, now, the cemeteries are filling up. You watch television when you can and you'll see probably a dozen funeral processions every morning. It's just awful!"

"What about you? Are you safe?"

"So far, yes, as you can see.

"Each of us nurses—there are twenty of us at last count—wears a mask and we're tested for infection every four hours. Even though we wear Latex gloves, we're required to wash our hands at least every half-hour. But, last week, a nurse from the second floor came down with Covid 19. She died three days later."

* * *

Zhang Wei's wife, he soon discovered, was doing quite well for herself. She had acquired a half-interest in the *Chop Suey Emporium*, one of Chinatown's busiest restaurants and she owned a three-unit apartment complex at 4791 Stockton Street, in the heart of Chinatown, with underground parking for the occupants. Its street-level, three-bedroom unit would be the couple's home for as long as they wished. Just being with her once more, after a separation of too many years, brought back a flood of memories, some pleasant, others not so.

Like Zhang Wei, Yu Yan Ying was born some 500 kilometers from the center of Beijing, in the village of Daio Pyong. Three years younger than Zhang Wei, her parents thought of her as 'a mistake,' this during the time when Mao Zedong ran the nation with an iron fist and had decreed that Chinese parents give birth to only one child, preferably a boy. More than once her parents talked about sending their infant child to an orphanage. But by the time she had reached age six, her parents realized they had a precocious child and they were determined to give her all the attention she deserved.

When Yu Yan was sixteen, she began dating a few of her classmates, one of them, Wang Xiu Li, was a friend of her sister playing on the same soccer team. Late one Saturday evening she returned to her home in tears, telling her parents that she'd been raped by Wang Xiu. The parents reported the event to the local police precinct captain who refused to become involved, saying that with teenagers this happens all too frequently, it becomes a 'she said, he said' affair with no way to establish guilt: was it really rape, or consensual sex?

**\* \* \***

The couple decided to have breakfast together in Yu Yan's modest kitchen alcove. What Zhang Wei learned during their conversation was at once surprising and mostly unpleasant.

One of his wife's tenants is a teenager, sixteen, Li Xiu Ying. He lives alone in the smallest of her several apartments and comes and goes at all hours. One week ago he confessed to Yu Yan that he has become an addict, but he can't shake the habit, try as he might. She recommended that he seek counselling but he refused, saying he doesn't want to embarrass his family. How does he acquire these drugs? Li Xiu refused to name his source but he did say the person is probably known to Yu Yan because he lives just down the street. He's a 26 year old Chinese-American, a citizen, and he has his own driver license. This unnamed person uses his car—a well-worn 1997 Volkswagen Beetle—to drive to the city's Pier 67 terminal, there to meet one of the city's rapidly-dwindling Mafioso adherents. We can call him Luigi. Luigi knows his customer is on his way because he's heard from him by cell phone. This gives Luigi time to scramble aboard a Panamanian-flagged freighter, the *Caribbean Cruiser*, and with a twenty dollar bill bribe the ship's single watchman. Then, with a hand truck, he brings to dockside as many as ten cases of bananas. In each of these cases, carefully concealed among the bananas, are as many as one hundred one-ounce packets of processed heroin; street value, $100 per packet, or $10,000 per case and $100,000 for the entire lot. As it is sold to street addicts, such as Li Xiu Ying, forty percent of the sales price flows back to Luigi who, when the entire lot has been sold, is now richer by $40,000, enough to buy a much better car, after selling his Beetle.

*   *   *

After telling her story, Yu Yan ended it with a bittersweet ending. Both Li Xiu Ying and the about to be identified Luigi have contracted Covid 19—most likely from the watchman or another crew member, and have been hospitalized at St. Mary's, each in that facility's ICU. Only a few hours earlier, she had notified a police officer and after hearing her story the officer told her it would be well to try to save both patients. The man known as Luigi would be able to identify the crew member, or members, of the ship and this should lead to an investigation of the heroin-smuggling operation and, perhaps, shut it down.

# FIVE

*Thursday, January 2, 2020, in the office of Terry Bradford, United States embassy, Beijing. Bradford is speaking to his assistant, James Wilkinson.*

"Jim, I've been thinking about that visitor we had yesterday, Zhang Wei Ying. Any day now, he should be on his way to San Francisco to join his wife who lives there. And that bothers me a bit."

"How so, Terry?"

"You'll recall that Zhang Wei was quite critical of Beijing's response to the Coronavirus outbreak in Wuhan. And he didn't seem to mind who knew about his opinions."

"Yes I do remember that. He was quite outspoken with his views. An it's certain that those sentiments have been recorded with the local intelligence people."

"That's right. I would bet a lot of money that the MSS has picked up on this and, if so, they aren't liking it. If Zhang Wei were still here, he'd be hauled in for interrogation as a traitor and probably jailed."

"So, we should notify Washington?"

"Correct. Eventually, this will be a matter for the FBI, but our channel goes through the State Department, its Office of Security."

**\*  \*  \***

*Special Agent George Morton of the FBI's San Francisco Field Office has secured an appointment with Yu Yan and is seated in her living room. Zhang Wei, her husband, is seated alongside. After introductions and a few pleasantries, he gets to the point.*

"As you two probably know, the FBI has what it calls a counter-intelligence function. That is to say it's our job to know about representatives of foreign nations who are in this country, some legally, some not. The Chinese government has an office here in San Francisco, a large one, and in that group are at least five officers of their intelligence service, the MSS or Ministry of State Security - - -"

"Uh, excuse me Mr. Morton, but what has this to do with us?"

"Yes. My office has received word that your husband, before coming to San Francisco, was openly critical of the way Chinese authorities in Beijing responded to the events in Wuhan, so much so that if he were still living in China, his life would be in danger."

"Oh, my!"

"Yes, and that's why I'm telling you this. You should be very careful about the people with whom you associate and, most important, avoid any contact with Chinese officials. As I said, several of them are intelligence officers, working here under cover as legitimate diplomats. You can assume they know who you are and where you live.

"I'm going to leave now. Here's my card and do feel free to call at any time."

\* \* \*

George Morton's warning could not have been more prescient. That very day, in the basement of the CPR's San Francisco Consulate General, two MSS officers—Heng Bo Hui and Ye Ru Yong—were re-reading a classified message just received from MSS headquarters in Beijing.

"So, Comrade Hui, we now have the address and phone number of the traitor Zhang Wei Ying. He's living with his wife in an apartment building on 4791 Stockton Street."

"Yes, Comrade Yong. That address is in the center of what the Americans refer to as Chinatown. It suggests that this family wishes to be well positioned, as the Americans would say, to stay in touch with everyone and everything.

"But, we must remember that our mission is not to assassinate the traitor, merely to warn him that he could die if we learn that he is spreading more malicious gossip about the unfortunate events in Wuhan."

"How do you propose we do this?"

"As you know, we have two surveillance teams on staff. I personally have trained one of them and I know they are very good at what they do, especially when they are working in this so-called Chinatown. They blend in with everyone else, they can appear as tourists, businessmen, salesmen, whatever we wish.

"But we must act quickly. Only yesterday California's governor said he will order all restaurants, bars and nightclubs to close on Monday, this in response to the so-called Coronavirus pandemic that has come upon us. We know our target likes to patronize the Chop Suey Emporium because his wife has a financial interest in that enterprise. I will arrange to meet him there, in person, assuming he will visit before the place closes."

*  *  *

And that is what happened. In anticipation of its closure, Zhang Wei and his wife decided to have one more meal, together, at their favorite restaurant. No sooner had they ordered, than Heng Bo Hui introduced himself as a representative of the MSS, claimed to know all about the couple's *treachery* and threatened to publish their names and photographs in Beijing's leading newspaper, identifying the two as traitors to the Motherland who had avoided due punishment by fleeing to the United States.

The next morning, the visibly shaken couple talk about how to respond.

"Yu Yan, that MSS officer never did say what he expects us—me, mostly—to do to avoid his threatened punishment."

"You're right. He didn't. But he probably expects you to sort of disappear, don't make waves, that sort of thing."

"Well, I didn't come all the way to San Francisco to be intimidated by what amounts to a threat. You know as well as I do that I—we—hope to be able to make a difference, here in our community and, possibly, throughout the country."

# SIX

The next morning, Zhang Wei and Yu Yan had breakfast together. After clearing the table, they retired to her small sitting room. She had decided to ask her husband for some advice about something that had been troubling her.

"Sweetheart, you've probably met Ye Ru Yong. He's one of my tenants, he's single, in his early forties, lives alone in one of my smaller apartments."

"I have met him but don't really know him. Why do you ask?"

"Well, after watching his comings and goings for some time, I'm pretty sure he's pimping for one of our city's brothels. It's the hours he keeps and the kind of visitors he brings home with him."

"What kind of visitors?"

"Prostitutes, almost certainly. You can tell by the way they dress, the kind of makeup they use."

"Well, as long as he pays his rent and doesn't bother the neighbors, what can you do about it?"

"It's the reputation of my business that worries me. You know how people talk. If the neighbors conclude that one of my tenants is a pimp, and that I know it, where does that leave me?"

"Prostitution is illegal in this city, right?"

"Yes, has been for years."

"So, you have every right to report this to the San Francisco police."

"I've done that, once. One of the precinct officers who patrols this neighborhood heard my story - - -"

"And?"

"He laughed and told me that his boss, the precinct captain, knows all about this. He has a deal with Ye Ru. So long as everything is quiet and nobody complains, the captain gets thirty percent of the brothel's income. Can you imagine?!"

"What about the hookers? Do they know?"

"If they do, they don't seem to care. He told me the average john pays $200 per trick, sometimes more. There are ten girls so it's a busy place with lots of customers.

"But, here's what's bothering me most about this."

"Tell me."

"One of the hookers, and I haven't yet learned her name, contracted Covid 19. You can imagine the possibilities: no masks, two naked bodies, enclosed in a very small room. She's now a patient at St.

Mary's Mercy Hospital, in its ICU, and the attending physician expects her to die within the next two days. There are four others, whose names I don't know, who are likely to be released within the next ten days.

"If there's anything good about this story, it's this. The officer who told me the story said they have an arrest warrant for Ye Ru Yong and it will be served tomorrow morning. He's pretty sure that when it goes to trial, the judge will sentence Ye Ru to no less than five years, with no time off for good behavior. The judge, he said, has seen this before and she wants to send a message that Chinatown's residents can't ignore."

# SEVEN

As often happens, their conversation turned to politics. Although Washington, DC is a long way from San Francisco, both had learned that what happens in the nation's capital can have a serious impact on what happens throughout the nation. As a successful entrepreneur, Yu Yan's experiences had influenced her political choices. She considered herself to be a rock-solid Conservative and she didn't mind talking about it, hoping to convert others. She was particularly distressed by the fact that two of the Bay Area's elected representatives were what she thought of as 'unrepentant liberals.' One of these woman, Norma Peterson, had become the Speaker of the House of Representatives, third in line to the presidency. The other, senator Debra Fisher, was the ranking member of the Senate's Judiciary committee and vice chair of The Senate's Intelligence committee.

Together, these two women had amassed a small fortune, not just in their Wall Street portfolios, but in their influence on the nation's future. What particularly galled Yu Yan, was Norma Peterson's stated intention to require the nation-wide closing of all K thru 12 schools, junior colleges and universities, 'non-essential' businesses, restaurants, bars, even barber shops and ladies' salons. If the congress went along, most of San Francisco's business community would cease to function, thousands of men and women would be furloughed from their jobs. As she thought about it, it reminder her of the stories of the 1930s Great Depression: soup kitchens, long lines of unemployed men and women begging for food, nine out of ten businesses filing for bankruptcy protection, underfunded Red Cross shelters for the homeless.

And in the White House, the mercurial president Owen Oglethorpe, although himself an outspoken Conservative, seemed to be yielding to the pressures of the Far Left, fearing that if he resisted it would damage his chances for re-election.

And, so it happened. In the House, the vote was 280 to 255 and in the Senate, 59 to 40 with one abstention. After the usual reconciliation process between the two bodies, the law became effective fifteen days later.

★  ★  ★

Although the state of California, to its detractors, had for years been referred to as part of 'The Left Coast,' (together with Oregon and Washington), two years earlier its citizens elected a Republic governor, third generation Mexican-American José Lopez. From his office in Sacramento, the governor let it be known that he was not about to adhere to the new law. He directed his Attorney General, Victor McGovern, to file a petition with California's Ninth Circuit Court of Appeals, demanding injunctive relief from the new law. As is usually the case with the Ninth Circuit, only one of its sitting justices heard the appeal, Republican Justice Margaret Wilson, and after a brief hearing she ruled in favor of the appeal.

★  ★  ★

When they heard the news, Zhang Wei and Yu Yan invited their neighbors—as many as could be squeezed into their apartment—for a celebration that extended far into the night. The gathering rivaled a typical Chinese New Year event. The implications were obvious. The city's businesses would remain open, the same for all the schools and universities, 'social distancing' and wearing protective masks was now voluntary, not required. The obvious downside: increased risks of spreading Covid 19.

Governor Lopez, well aware of this threat, asked the state legislature to approve an emergency appropriation of $1,000,000 grants-in-aid to each hospital that was treating Coronavirus patients, the money to be used only for ventilators and other devices unique to treating those patients known to be at risk.

* * *

Before retiring for the night, Zhang Wei told his wife he had decided to apply for a California license to practice medicine. He reasoned that with enough time, his study and research would prepare him to pass the required examinations. He added that he was quite certain that, in the long term, he could make a significant difference in America's struggle with the Coronavirus epidemic.

# EIGHT

Following Bishop Wagner's retirement, the Catholic hierarchy appointed Fr. James Kincaid to the position. Ten days after his confirmation, he began Monday through Friday radio broadcasts on one of San Francisco's FM station, KCYA, and established his own Web page. His listeners/viewers soon realized that Fr. Kincaid considered himself to be something of a biblical scholar, especially in his studies of the Old Testament. He spoke of God's decision to cause a great flood, to punish His people for their unrepentant sinning and He instructed Noah to build a great ark, so that humankind and animals would be spared.

He spoke of God's supernatural powers over all the earth, as when it was darkened for three hours, following Jesus' death on the cross (Mt. 27:45).

He went on to say that he believed the current Coronavirus pandemic was God's way of punishing His sinful people that, in spite of His unconditional love for all humankind, He had decided that the pandemic was the only way to remind people of His infinite power and that He would end the pandemic only when and if His children came to repentance.

* * *

Although neither Zhang Wei nor his wife had ever subscribed to Catholicism, Yu Yan did, occasionally, listen to Fr. Kincaid's messages. She owed her job, at least indirectly, to the Catholic Church, and thought it wise to listen to what its leaders had to say. The two were finishing lunch when Kincaid's most recent message ended.

"What do you think, Sweetheart? Does what we just heard make sense?"

"Yu Yan, that may be the wrong question. It doesn't matter if it makes sense. What matters is how many of his listeners believe it? Personally, I can't believe it. I couldn't believe it even if I were a member of the Church. But I read somewhere that there are more than 70 million Catholics in this country and it's what *they* believe that matters. And I can see possibilities for a schism to develop, if enough people have heard or read about what we just heard. Protestants and, even, non-believers, blaming Catholics for their unbelief, this being responsible for the pandemic. Or, the other way around. A lot of finger pointing throughout a society that can ill afford it."

"Any ideas?"

"Yes, definitely. You and I and as many others as we can persuade, we write letters and make phone calls and insist that Fr. Kincaid stop what he's doing. He really has no credentials with which to support his opinions. I suspect it may be nothing more than an over-inflated ego that's responsible."

* * *

And, so it was. The phone calls and letters were persuasive and within six weeks Fr. Kincaid's ideas were removed from circulation. But, it gave serious pause to Zhang Wei's thoughts about his own future. Instead of being an outside observer—as he was now—he would be more effective if he could participate from the *inside*. And for that, he decided, he should apply for a position in his wife's hospital. Most of its patients lived in Chinatown and Mandarin was his native tongue. Surely, there he could make a difference.

\* \* \*

But wait. No sooner had he told Yu Yan about his decision, she referred him to a recent article in *The Wall Street Journal*. Its author, a senator serving on the Senate's Select Intelligence Committee, wrote this:

"The U.S. government is investigating whether the Covid 19 virus came from a government laboratory in Wuhan, China. The Chinese Communist Party denies the possibility. 'There is no way this virus came from us,' claimed Yuan Zhiming over the weekend. Mr. Yuan is a top researcher in the Wuhan Institute of Virology, which studies some of the world's deadliest pathogens. He is also secretary of the lab's Communist Party committee. He accuses me of 'deliberately trying to mislead the people' for suggesting his laboratory as a possible origin for the pandemic.

'Beijing has claimed that the virus originated in a Wuhan *wet market*, where wild animals were sold. But evidence to the counter this theory emerged in January. Chinese researchers reported in *The Lancet* (January 24) that the first known cases had no contact with the market, and Chinese state media acknowledged the finding. There's no evidence the market sold bats or pangolins, the animals from which the virus is thought to have jumped to humans. And the bat species that carries it isn't found within 100 miles of Wuhan.

'Wuhan has two labs where we know bats and humans interacted. One is the Institute of Virology, eight miles from the market, the other is the Wuhan Center for Disease Control and Prevention, barely 300 yards from the market.

'Both labs collect wild animals to study viruses. Their researchers travel to caves across China to capture bats for this purpose. Chinese state media released a minidocumentary in mid-December following a team of Wuhan CDC researchers collecting live bats in caves. The researchers fretted openly about the risk of infection.

'These risks were not limited to the field. *The Washington Post* reported last week that in 2018 U.S. diplomats in China warned of 'a serious shortage of appropriately trained technicians and investigators needed to safely operate' the Institute of Virology. The Wuhan CDC operates at even lower biosafety standards.

'While the Chinese government denies the possibility of a lab leak, its actions tell a different story. The Chinese military posted its top epidemiologist to the institute of Virology in January. In February, chairman Xi Jinping urged swift implementation of new biosafety rules to govern pathogens in laboratory settings. Academic papers about the virus's origins are now subject to prior restraint by the government.

'In early January enforcers threatened doctors who warned their colleagues about the virus. Among them was Li Wenliang, who died of Covid 19 in February. Laboratories working to sequence the virus's genetic code were ordered to destroy their samples. The laboratory that first published virus's genome was shut down, Hong Kong's *South China Morning Post* reported in February.

'To be sure, the evidence is circumstantial, but it all points to toward the Wuhan labs. Thanks to the Chinese coverup, we may never have direct, conclusive evidence—intelligence rarely works that way—but

Americans justifiably can use common sense to follow the inherent logic of events to their likely conclusions.'

*   *   *

"What do you think, Sweetheart? This is a much different story from what we've heard up to now."

"It has that ring of truth, no doubt, and we both know about the Chinese leaders' capacity for deception. What the author didn't say, but what makes sense to me, is that that laboratory was trying to develop a *weapon*, a weapon of an entirely different nature, one for which the world has no defense."

"Well, now we know it's not going to happen.

"Another subject. I've decided to apply for a license to practice medicine, here in California. I've done some online research and I know what the examinations require. They're posted in English but that shouldn't be a problem. There's a filing fee, which I can handle with a credit card and after that's accepted, I can take the exam online, using my laptop. And with the governor's *Stay Home* order, the laptop will be just fine.

It takes about three hours and the office in Sacramento promises to return the results within a week. Then, I'm required to go to the nearest hospital and interview with one of its resident physicians. If he/she signs off, then I'm good to go!"

# NINE

After hearing her husbands plans, Yu Yan thought she might help. It was one thing to study for and the pass all the required tests, but what then? Her husband would have to intern at a hospital for one year and he would surely choose St. Mary's Mercy to do that. And knowing the right people would help. Yes, she knew Li Xiu Ying, the Chinese-American physician who had the day shift at St. Mary's and his wife, Chen Bao, presently the head nurse in the hospital's ICU.

She knew about the old American saying, *It's not what you know, but WHO you know* and knowing these two would be a big help. She picked up her iPhone and called Chen Bao. Yes, they would be free Saturday evening and, yes, they would love to have dinner with Yu Yan and her husband.

* * *

The dinner was a huge success. Yu Yan served *Laziji*, a favorite with most Chinese: a combination of boned chicken, lightly roasted; chili bean paste. pepper, garlic and vinegar, served on a bed of brown rice, with a side dish of blanched asparagus tips in Hollandaise sauce. After loading the dishwasher, the four retired to Yu Yan's living room. The propane fireplace was already aglow. She had spoken, earlier, with Zhang Wei about 'what to drink,' after the meal. He suggested *Wuliangye*, a popular liquor made from fermented rice and crushed hazel nuts, alcohol content about 90%. The two realized that to promote easy and unrestrained conversation, an ounce of two of *Wuliangye* might be necessary.

It was and it worked. Before the two guests retired for the evening, Li Xiu invited Zhang Wei to come to his hospital office first thing Monday morning. There, he explained, he had a small adjoining office and this would be Zhang Wei's 'workshop' for as long as it took to get him ready for his online examinations. He would have free access to the entire hospital, its staff and senior administrators. Further, his wife Chen Bao would be available to introduce Zang Wei to the hospital's female nurses, some sixty of them.

**\* \* \***

As he thought about it later, Zhang Wei marveled at the working environment in which he found himself. Most of the people he worked with were bilingual, speaking either English or Mandarin, whichever language was needed at the moment. The staff, somehow, managed to observe the 'social distancing' protocol, staying at least six feet from each other, while wearing the hospital-approved white gowns and face masks. The hospital's cafeteria had been reconfigured so that each table, seating four, kept the diners separated by the prescribed distance, allowing them to remove their masks while eating.

The rules were more difficult to follow in the hospital's several wards. The physicians in charge of wards one, two and three—where the majority of patients were cared for—insisted that patients and all hospital employees wear the proper mask and Latex gloves. But in ward four, where the Covid-19 cases were cared for, the rules were even more confining: absolutely NO visitors, portable ventilators for those patients who needed them, a physician walk-through every 30 minutes, all of this 24/7.

*   *   *

On day ten of his introduction to the hospital's routines, Zhang Wei met with his mentor, Li Xiu Ying. The two men chatted about procedures and the rules and agreed that Zhang Wei was learning about as quickly as could be expected. But, now it was time for the student to experience what every licensed physician was going through: tomorrow, beginning at eight a.m., follow Li Xiu as he makes his rounds.

On schedule, the two men met at eight and began at the entrance to ward four, each of them wearing the prescribed pure white gown and face mask. There were twenty Covid-19 patients, ten on each side of the ward, each one connected to a ventilator and a chart attached to the foot of each bed. For Li Xiu, it was a routine he had mastered days earlier, examining the chart and deciding if the patient was in recovery mode or about to perish. If the latter, he made a note on the chart, requesting that the city's funeral home services be notified, also the nearest morgue.

"You know, Zhang Wei, this is the toughest part of my job, making decisions like this. What if I'm wrong? The patient recovers enough to go home and the family sues the hospital, or me."

"You have insurance, don't you?"

"Sure, liability. But only up to a million. Some of these lawsuits ask three times that much, and there's nothing we can do about it."

*   *   *

Ten days later, after breakfast, Zhang Wei knew he wasn't feeling well; sore throat, congested lungs, loss of taste and smell and a slight fever. 'Hmm, so it's finally happening to *me,* Covid-19. That's what I get for making those hospital rounds with Li Xiu. I'll give him a call and tell him I'm going into self-quarantine, fourteen days."

Much to his surprise, Zhang Wei felt perfectly normal after the first week. He decided to return to the hospital and tell Li Xiu the good news.

"You say you're okay? After only one week?"

"That's right, Friend. I've never felt better."

"Zhang Wei, this is *most* unusual. If you don't mind I'd like to draw a small blood sample. We can look at it, together, with our electron microscope."

"You have one of *those*? How much did you pay for it?"

"Yes, normally one of these will retail for about a million dollars. We bought a used one for about half that, one of our wealthy San Francisco donors paid for most of it."

"Let's step into our lab and have a look. Ours has two viewers so we can sit side by side while we're looking at the same thing."

It took a few minutes for everything to be made ready. Then

"Okay, Zhang Wei, this is what one of your blood cells looks like. The scope is set to enlarge the image by a factor of 100,000. I've looked at lot of these over the years and I can see there's something different about this sample."

"What is it?"

"Yes. If you look carefully at the lower right-corner of the cell, you'll see a tiny object, kind of a green translucent color."

"I see it."

"I'd bet a month's salary that that—it's likely one of the cell's proteins—has given your system an immunity to the Coronavirus."

"Really!?"

"Yes, I'm quite sure of it. So the question now is, can you remember ever being exposed, say years ago?"

"Yes, I can. Before I left Beijing to come here, I spent two days in my hotel room, same symptoms as now: headache, congested lungs, slight fever. But those symptoms disappeared and I felt fine."

"Okay, that rounds the circle. That is how you became immune to the Coronavirus.

"By the way, what's your blood type?"

"B Positive. Why do you ask?"

"Perfect. So is mine. Now, if you agree, we'll try something that, to my knowledge, has never been done before."

"Sort of like pioneering medicine?"

"Exactly. If you'll sit right where you are and roll up a sleeve, I'm going to inject a few drops of your blood into my bloodstream. Within ten minutes or so we'll know if my idea works."

*Ten minutes later*

"Now, we put a drop of my blood under the scope and have a look. If that same green translucent blob appears, then we'll know that I, too, am immune to the Coronavirus."

"Hmm, I'd have to say you're a genius, Li Xiu. It's there, all right, just like you thought it would be. Now what?"

"That was the easy part, Zhang Wei. Now we need to find a way to synthesize that little green monster. If we, or someone else, can do that, we'll have a vaccine that could, in time, put an end to this pandemic."

# TEN

Yu Yan was returning from her eight-hour shift at the hospital when she stopped at a newspaper kiosk not far from her apartment building. Both she and her husband were trying to follow the nation's political developments, mostly by watching television but occasionally by reading newspapers. They soon discovered that most readers considered the three best to be *The Wall Street Journal,* the, *New York Times* and *The Washington Post.* They had grown to prefer the *Journal,* owing to its usually-conservative articles and editorials. But before leaving the hospital, one of her co-workers suggested she pick up a copy of the *Washington Post.* On its editorial page was a long article about China, written by a former presidential candidate, a conservative Republican.

*   *   *

"America is awakening to China. The covid-19 pandemic has revealed that, to a great degree, our very health is in Chinese hands; from medicines to masks, we are at Beijing's mercy. Embarrassed by the revelation of this vulnerability, politicians in Washington will certainly act to remedy our medical dependence — with the usual fanfare and self-congratulation. But China's stranglehold on pharmaceuticals is only a small sliver of its grand strategy for economic, military and geopolitical domination. The West's response must extend much further — it will require a unified strategy among free nations to counter China's trade predation and its corruption of our mutual security.

"In recent years, China has succeeded in disproportionately positioning its citizens and proxies with loyalties to the Chinese Communist Party in key international governing bodies, allowing it to expand its geopolitical influence. China relentlessly badgers and bribes nations to avert their leaders' eyes from its egregious abuses of Uighurs, Tibetans, and other minorities — as well as its targeting pro-democracy leaders in Hong Kong. The same methods result in the geopolitical isolation of Taiwan. All the while, China spreads pacifying propaganda throughout the world; even right under our noses, so-called Confucius Institutes peddle pro-China messages in America's colleges and high schools.

"China's alarming military build-up is not widely discussed outside classified settings, but Americans should not take comfort in our disproportionately large military budget. The government of President Xi Jinping doesn't report its actual defense spending. An apples-to-apples analysis demonstrates that China's annual procurement of military hardware is nearly identical to ours; but because our military has missions around the world, this means that in the Pacific, where China concentrates its firepower, it will have military superiority. No wonder the Philippines and other Pacific nations have cozied up to their powerful neighbor.

"Today, however, Beijing's weapon of choice is economic: The tip of its spear is global industrial predation. China not only steals technology from other nations, it massively subsidizes industries it determines to have strategic importance. Further, it employs competitive practices that have long been forbidden by developed nations, including bribery, monopoly, currency manipulation and predatory pricing.

"As China ascended in the global marketplace, the West indulged its aberrant industrial policies, hoping it would move toward freedom and adherence to the international rules of commerce. That indulgence exacted a heavy toll. For example, China achieved a breathtaking capture of the global steel market through means that are illegal or impossible elsewhere: pricing far below cost, artificially depressing currency, massive government subsidies and, to be sure, a measure of bribes. Between 2000 and 2009, China more than tripled its global share of steel production, and now it controls more than half of the world's output — resulting in steel plants shuttered around the globe and the sacrifice of hundreds of thousands of jobs.

"China employs its predatory tools across the economy, from high-tech and national security sectors of nanotechnology, telecommunications and artificial intelligence to basic mining and manufacturing. A Chinese conglomerate recently acquired a dominant Indonesian stainless steel company. Indonesia just happens to be the largest producer of the world's nickel, an essential ingredient in the production of stainless steel. Suddenly, Indonesia has agreed to shut off nickel exports to any of China's foreign competitors. Another near-monopoly is born, thanks to anti-competitive tactics.

"When a predator, unbound by the rules followed by its competitors, is allowed to operate in a free market, that market is no longer truly free.

"As a first step, the president was right to blow the whistle on Beijing and apply tariffs. But we must go a good deal further. We must align our negotiating strategy and policies with other nations that adhere to the global rules of trade. This means narrowing trade disputes with our friends and uniting against China's untethered abuse. China must understand that it will not have free, unfettered access to any of our economies unless it ceases to employ anti-competitive and predatory practices. It will face a simple choice: Play by the global rules, or face steep economic penalties.

"Further action should be applied in national security sectors such as artificial intelligence, telecommunication and, as we now know, pharmaceuticals. The free nations must collectively agree that we will buy these products only from other free nations. In addition to protecting our security, such an agreement would incentivize our research and industrial institutions to invest in these areas, knowing that they will not be undercut by Chinese predatory practices.

"China has done what we have allowed it to do; to save a few dollars, we have looked the other way. Covid-19 has exposed China's dishonesty for all to see. And it is a clarion call for America to seize the moment. When the immediate health crisis has passed, the United States should convene like-minded nations to develop a common strategy aimed at dissuading China from pursuing its predatory path."

*  *  *

The article so impressed Yu Yan that she asked her husband to read it and he, too, reacted the same way; perplexed, confused and, yes, angry. To realize that his former homeland had become the world's primary predator, and that, now, America was waking to that reality, required him to ask himself, 'What can I do about this, if anything?'

"What do you think, Sweetheart? Do we just ignore these painful truths, pretend we know nothing about them?"

"You know the expression; *No way, José!* First, we can ask everyone at the hospital to read this piece; not everyone will, of course, but for those who do we can organize small after-hours discussion groups, say five or six people at a time. We can write letters to the editor. Even though *The San Francisco Chronicle* is a Hearst-family liberal newspaper, its editors will recognize that a lot of people—especially Chinese-Americans—are really upset about this. And if we do this, it won't be long before others learn about it, maybe even a few newspaper reporters and television people."

"Yes, I agree with that, as I usually do. You're a bright woman, Yu Yan, but I'm thinking there's something else that we—I—can do that might be even more effective."

"And?- - -"

"Yes. If I were to persuade management to accept me as a member of the hospital's staff, I'd be able to have far more influence than I have right now. What do you think?"

"Wonderful. Let's do it!"

\* \* \*

Like many American hospitals, St. Mary's Mercy was an independently-owned and financed institution. It received no financial help from the federal government and relied entirely on donations from many of its wealthy patrons, many of them Chinese-Americans but not all. Another reliable supporter: the Catholic Archdiocese and its Board of Supervisors. And it was no secret that anyone who contributed money to support the hospital could list those gifts as charitable donations on his/her 1040 income tax reports to the IRS.

\* \* \*

George Eaton was the senior reporter for *The Wall Street Journal*'s five-man office in San Francisco. A thirty-year veteran, he'd worked for the *Journal* in such far-flung places as Moscow, Santiago, London, Paris and Shanghai. During his three years in the Chinese metropolis, he learned to speak Mandarin well enough to interview in both English and that language. Early one morning he received an email from his editor-in-chief in the *Journal*'s New York headquarters: *There's a story at Chinatown's St. Mary's Mercy Hospital. Get on it, please!*

\* \* \*

"Hey, Casey, that hospital in Chinatown, St. Mary's Mercy, that's part of your beat, isn't it.?

"Sure thing, George, I was over there yesterday."

"So, New York tells me there's a story we should know about. What say you?"

"Yeah, I was about to suggest the same thing. Kind of unusual, too. The hospital has just added a new physician to its staff and this guy is not just *any* physician. His name is Zhang Wei Ying, born in China, speaks both English and Mandarin, and in the past few days has become something of an expert on things having to do with the Coronavirus. I was told that he recently demonstrated that he's immune to the virus, as is one of his physician-colleagues. They claim to have found the source of the infection, a miniscule protein in the bloodstream's cell structure. Now they're hoping to figure a way to synthesize that protein and if they can do that, they'll have produced the first vaccine to prevent Covid-19. Of course that's too much of a challenge for a few physicians, so they're hoping to attract investors to finance the research."

"Like a new startup?"

"Most likely. But they'll need to patent the process if they want have exclusive rights. And I was told they're in the process of doing that, as we speak."

# ELEVEN

*Three days later this article appeared in the Journal's U.S. News section, page 3.*

## SAN FRANCISCO
Promising Coronavirus Developments
By Casey Williams

The staff at St. Mary's Mercy hospital, in central Chinatown, may be on to something. Informed sources tell me that one of its interns, Dr. Zhang Wei Ying, has developed a technique for identifying the Coronavirus cell in the human bloodstream. It is a unique protein that is found *only* in those patients who are immune to the virus. Dr. Ying contracted a mild case of Covid-19 when he was in Beijing, at the time of the first outbreak in Wuhan in late December. That exposure, he says, is what produced the immune protein. He and a few co-workers are applying for a patent which, if approved, will lead to the synthesis of the protein and the development of an effective vaccine.

Dr. Ying is incorporating himself and three colleagues in a startup firm to be known as *Covid Control*. After filing the necessary paperwork, Covid Control will be listed on the Nasdaq exchange and once a share price has been set, readers are invited to participate.

**\* \* \***

The following morning, president Oglethorpe's press secretary—after reading the WSJ article—urged the president to read it himself. The president's detractors had accused him of being too slow in his response to the Coronavirus pandemic. But if he were to endorse the news from San Francisco and urge nationwide support of Dr. Ying's program, his detractors might be silenced. After hearing this suggestion, the president agreed, but *only* if Dr. Ying would agree to come to Washington, meet with the president and appear on television.

**\* \* \***

It was a no-brainer for Zhang Wei. Of course he would go to Washington and of course he would insist that his wife accompany him. Their appearance on television would surely promote their ideas about stopping the pandemic. And it would give them the opportunity to persuade president Oglethorpe to support their program, to encourage people to invest in Covid Control. Sure, other pharmaceutical companies are scrambling to develop a vaccine, but that's the American way, plenty of competition.

They chose the Willard Intercontinental Hotel as was within walking distance of the White House and the president's invitation had included a voucher that would cover the cost, $246 per night, up to four nights. It added that the same voucher could be used to hire a rental car, should the couple wish to do some sightseeing while in the Washington vicinity.

\* \* \*

Their TV appearance was held in the West Wing's library, with television crews from NBC, ABC, CBS and Fox News and PBS' *World News Today* video-recording the event. It was aired in prime time, 8 p.m. Eastern and 5 p.m. Pacific. PBS chose to rebroadcast at noon the following day.

Although some of assembled reporters complained, the president insisted there be no questions following his remarks. He said it would unfair to subject his guests—new to American ways—to what might appear to be hostile inquiries..

\* \* \*

President Oglethorpe began with a statement, read from his teleprompter.

"Ladies and Gentlemen, it is my pleasure to introduce to you two remarkable Americans, Doctor Zhang Wei Ying and his lovely wife Yu Yan. Both were born in China and have since moved to San Francisco's Chinatown where they are employed at St. Mary's Mercy hospital. That hospital, like every hospital, is treating patients suffering from Covid-19, the disease borne by the novel Coronavirus. When I said *remarkable*, I did so intentionally. Dr. Ying was infected with the virus while he was in Beijing, not that long ago, and has since discovered himself to be immune to the disease. He and a co-worker, also immune, are seeking to patent a process which, if successful, will lead to the creation and mass production of a vaccine which will negate the Coronavirus's ability to infect people.

"As you know, presidents are not expected to endorse commercial ventures but, in this case, I'm making an exception, owing to the urgency of the matter. I have sent a message to the Nasdaq Exchange, urging them to accept Dr. Ying's proposal for an Initial Public Offering for his new corporation, *Covid Control*. And if those of you who are watching or listening should so desire, I would encourage you to consider purchasing shares; I understand the opening price will be announced later today.

"Thank you."

* * *

The next morning Covid Control opened at $12.00 per share (on sales of 83,333 shares, nearly half of which were purchased by banks and other institutions in the San Francisco Bay area) and at the three o'clock bell the Nasdaq posted $23.50, nearly double the price of its opening, a total of nearly $2,000,000.00. After the Nasdaq's two percent surcharge, Covid Control found itself worth $1,960,000.

Zhang Wei had opened a business account at the Chinatown branch of First Federal of California and one phone call to the bank's manager told him the money had already been deposited, a wire transfer from Nasdaq. He had decided who should be part of his Board of Directors: his wife: Wang Xiu Li, the physician in charge of the hospital's Covid 19 recovery wing; Li Xiu Ying, one of the hospital's junior physicians and his nurse-wife, Chen Bao, the head nurse in the hospital's ICU. Each of the four, when approached, had agreed to serve without compensation for the first six months of their contract. Beyond that, their remunerations would be in the range of five percent of the corporation's profits.

* * *

From his hotel room, Zhang Wei used his iPhone to talk to Li Xiu and catch up on the hospital staff's reactions to the news. He wasn't surprised to learn that they were 'dancing in the hallways,' as Li Xiu put it.

# TWELVE

*In the Oval Office, president Oglethorpe is speaking to his Center for Disease Control advisor, Dr. William Curtis. Curtis has flown to Washington, from Atlanta, at the president's request.*

"Bill, I've just received a faxed aerial photograph from our friends at NSA. You'll recall that three weeks ago I called in the Chinese ambassador—Wong Chi Fang—and insisted that his government shut down that lab in Wuhan, the one where this pandemic got its start."

"I do remember that, Mr. President. Why do you mention it?"

"Because this photograph from NSA, and the attached photo interpretation report, tells me the Chinese haven't done what I insisted they do. The lab is still going full blast, as you can tell from the vehicle traffic that comes and goes. If you were my shoes, what would *you* do?"

"I'd recall the ambassador and tell him that if the Chinese refuse to comply, you'll give the story to every media outlet in the country. They know that we suspect the Coronavirus escaped from that very laboratory and the fact that they refuse to close it tells the world they don't care what president Oglethorpe says or thinks."

"That's exactly what I was thinking. I'll ask my press secretary to get on it."

* * *

*In Beijing, chairman Xi Jinping is speaking to his National Security advisor, General Wong Fu Ching.*

"General, what do you make of this threat from the White House? Are they serious?"

"I would say they're very serious, Comrade Xi. But there *is* a way around this threat."

"How so?"

"We can dismantle the lab and make it obvious. Their satellites will take pictures, proving that we've acceded to their demand. Then we wait, say, a month and the world will come to believe that the White House has prevailed.

"But during this pause, and only during hours of darkness, we ship the lab's components to those Longyou Caves, way out in Zhejiang Province. Along with the shipments we send the same technicians who worked at the Wuhan lab and within a month or six weeks everything will be as it was, only no one will know. Their NSA programmers will work on other targets and our facility should be able to operate indefinitely."

"General, I like that very much. Thank you!"

* * *

*After dismissing the general, Chairman Xi Jinping reached for his phone and asked to be connected to the Wuhan laboratory. And use the secure line.*

"Comrade Zhang, is that you?"

"Yes, of course, Sir. What can I do for you?"

"Comrade, are we secure?"

"Yes, Sir, absolutely."

"Good. You should know that your laboratory will be dismantled within the next few weeks. Before that unfortunate event occurs, I want to know how your *Project Y* is progressing."

"Everything is on schedule, Sir. The three technicians have been sworn to absolute secrecy. They know they're producing a weapon that is unique and, of course, quite effective.

"They have been able to capture very small amounts of the Coronavirus and insert them into a metal container about the size of a package of cigarettes. The container has an adhesive strip and when it is pressed against, say, the underside of a wash basin or a table in a restaurant, that activates a timing mechanism. Five minutes later, the pathogens are released in an invisible aerosol spray, thus infecting those patrons with the Coronavirus.

"Very good, Comrade! We can think of it as the ultimate weapon.

"Now, it is vital that those same technicians participate in the dismantling of your laboratory *and* that they accompany its components to the lab's new location, in the Longyou Caves in Zhejiang province. As you know, those caves are very large and can easily accommodate the same laboratory. If we move everything in total darkness, the American satellites won't be able to see what's happening.

"So, Comrade Zhang, you have your orders; and do not fail!"

*  *  *

*NSA Headquarters, Ft. Meade, Maryland. S/Sgt Jeremy Wilson's shift has ended and he welcomes his relief, Sgt. James Felton.*

"Hey, Jim, before I go I want you to look at something. You'll recall that we received a work order from the White House, not that long ago."

"Sure I remember. They want us to look at any photography that covers that Wuhan laboratory, the place where the Coronavirus pandemic got started."

"I just downloaded a time-lapse sequence to your monitor. If you look closely, you can see the lab is being dismantled: large, 4x4 trucks coming and going. The trucks are parked nearby and, finally, the whole structure has been loaded onto those trucks.

"But then, one day later, those same trucks move out. Only now, everything is at night and all you can see are the trucks' headlights. Part of that time-lapse sequence is happening with a full moon, so you can barely make out the outline of the trucks, rolling along at about 50 mph. As soon as it gets light, the trucks try to find cover, under a freeway overpass, or a large bridge. So it's pretty obvious that the Chinese are going to a heck of a lot of trouble to hide whatever they're doing."

"So what do we do with this? We can tell the White House what we're looking at but - -"

"No. I think we should shoot this whole thing over to our friends in Langley. The

CIA's photo interpreters are just as good as ours. They'll know what to do."

\* \* \*

*Far East Division chief Walter Jensen was the first to see NSA's Fax, along with some of the photographs. He has called in his deputy, John Grove.*

"John, this material from NSA really bugs me. For one, it proves the Chinese never intended to obey the president's demarche and they're being very sneaky about it."

"I'd agree with that, Walt, but for this to make sense we need to know *where* those trucks are going. My guess is they intend to set up that lab somewhere else."

"You're right, let's ask NSA to keep looking."

**\*  \*  \***

*Ten days later, Walter Jensen received the latest from NSA, this time without photos but a written memorandum addressed to Jensen.*

"Our satellite tracking has revealed what happened to those trucks in which you were interested. After leaving Wuhan, they proceeded— slowly, average 35 mph—all the way to the village of Longyou, the site of the entrance to the Longyou Caves. The GPS position is accurate to within 200 yards: Latitude 29.067325 north, longitude 119.186864 east. This was a 'stealth movement,' meaning that all travel was during hours of darkness, with only the vehicles' headlights visible. At a straight-line distance of 1,000 kilometers the journey required nearly three days to complete. Our photography shows that the trucks—15 of them—appear to have entered the caves. What their purpose is, we cannot say."

**\*  \*  \***

"John, I'm going to forward this message to our station in Beijing. They need to know what we know."

# FOURTEEN

*One of those three technicians, Lin Bo Yang, is speaking to his cousin, Dr. Ying Fu Yang.*

"Cousin Ying, I probably shouldn't be telling you this but - -"

"But what, Lin Bo?"

"You probably don't know this, but Beijing has ordered us to disassemble our Wuhan laboratory and transport it to the Longyou Caves in Zhejiang province. The American president is very upset about our work here in Wuhan and that's why we're moving. But we're doing it at night, so the American satellites won't see what's happening.

"But that's not the worst of it. My two coworkers and I have developed a means of releasing the Coronavirus pathogens in such a way that we can be selective about who becomes infected. One of our leaders calls it 'the ultimate weapon.' Once the laboratory is up and running in those caves, we're expected to manufacture up to 100 of those devices every day. They'll be used only by our intelligence service and the targets will be visiting foreigners, especially American tourists, in popular places like Shanghai, Beijing, Nanjing and X'ian.

"I've decided I don't want to be part of this scheme because I know that if it succeeds thousands—maybe more—innocent people will become ill with Covid-19 and many of them will die!"

"Yes, Lin Bo, I certainly agree with your concerns. And as an experienced physician this may trouble me more than it does you. It so happens that I have business to attend to in Beijing. While I'm there—assuming you agree—I'll go to the American embassy and tell them what you've just told me."

\* \* \*

*Six days later, in office of Jeffry Sheldon, the CIA's Chief of Station in Beijing. Sheldon is speaking to his deputy, Thomas Hoyt.*

"You know, Tom, what that Dr. Fu Yang told us may be the best psych war opportunity this agency has ever had."

"Amen to that, Jeff. He not only brought photographs but he left behind an exemplar of that Coronavirus dispenser. Fortunately, he assured us it's empty. But you gotta hand it to the guys who invented this thing; it looks exactly like a pack of cigarettes."

"I'm going to send this stuff to headquarters. There's a branch in the Far East division that specializes in psych warfare but they haven't had much opportunity to do anything with China, not since the pandemic got its start in Wuhan. Now, that's likely to change."

\* \* \*

*In the office of Walter Herness, Chief, Beijing Support branch, CIA headquarters.*

"Sally, would you ask Mark Jarvis to meet me in our conference room? He's our psych war specialist and this material from Beijing will give him something to work with."

*Fifteen minutes later.*

"Okay, Mark. You now know as much about this as I do. What do you make of it?"

"This is dynamite stuff, Walt. We should task our friends at NSA to have another look at the entrance to those caves. Only yesterday we learned—along with the rest of the world—that the caves have been closed 'indefinitely' as a tourist attraction and that in itself is suspicious. We now know that the Chinses intend to use those caves as a manufacturing facility for those little packages that are loaded with the Coronavirus."

"---And that they intend use them against foreign visitors, especially American visitors."

"But, before we go any further with this, the director likely will want to check in with the White House. Because when we pull the string, the entire Chinese leadership is going to have a lot of explaining to do."

"Maybe just the *threat* of pulling that string would be enough."

"Let's find out."

★　★　★

*Three days later in the Oval Office. President Oglethorpe is speaking to the Chinese ambassador to Washington, Lin Fu Wong.*

"Mr. Ambassador, I know your English is good enough that we don't need an interpreter to sit in on our conversation."

"Yes, Mr. President, that is correct. Thank you, Sir."

"My detractors claim I don't have a diplomatic bone in my body, and that is probably true. So, I'll get right to the point.

"My government, through its intelligence service, now has absolute proof about what is going on in those far-away Longyou Caves. Here is a recent satellite photograph of the entrance to those caves: many trucks coming and going, carrying various supplies.

"And I have, here in my hands, an exemplar of what those caves are producing, something like a package of cigarettes, a package loaded with the Coronavirus and intended for use against foreign visitors, including, Mr. Ambassador, *American* visitors!

"I'm told that your specialists consider this your *ultimate weapon*, to be used when, where and against whomever you wish."

"Uh, excuse me, Mr. President, but I honestly know nothing about this. Any project of this kind would be treated with the utmost secrecy. Surely, you can appreciate that!"

"That matters not to me, not at all. What *does* matter is that your government immediately put an end to this project.

"You can respond to my demands in one of two ways. You can ignore them or you can agree. If you choose the latter course, we can do this without publicity, not in my country. What happens in yours is up to you."

"Yes, Mr. President. I perfectly understand your position. Of course I must report our conversation to my superiors in Beijing. Given the urgency of the matter, I should expect a reply within 24 hours."

* * *

The reply was on time but it surprised everyone who saw it: 'Thanks, but no thanks, we'll take our chances.'

# FIFTEEN

*Two days later, Jeffry Sheldon, the CIA's Chief of Station in Beijing is speaking to his deputy, Thomas Hoyt.*

"Well, Tom, now that the Chinese have said, in effect, 'go fly a kite,' seems to me what we need are *photographs* of what's going on inside those caves. If we had a few of those, the Chinese would have to admit that our accusations are correct."

"I've been thinking the same thing, Jeff, and it brings to mind that sleeper agent of ours. I haven't talked to him for at least six months— there's been no need to—but now it might be time."

"You're talking about the physician, Yin Fu Wong?"

"One and the same. Ever since that blowup in the Wuhan lab, he's been very concerned about where this is going and, more than that, he thinks the Beijing leadership is led by a bunch of no-nothing zealots. So his motivation couldn't be better."

"What's he doing these days?"

"He's now one of the three leading immunologists in Beijing's hospital system. He knows as much about the Coronavirus as anyone. He and I touch base now and then with our cell phones; a couple of weeks ago he told me he's bored and would like to have something better to do."

"Would he be willing to go to those caves, try to get a job there?"

"I believe he would. But I need to check a couple of files before we go any further."

* * *

*An hour later.*

"Here it is, Jeff. The name of one of the three techs who were on duty when the Wuhan lab made front page news, Dr. Wan Fu Yang; age 35, single. I'd bet a week's wages he's already on duty in those caves."

"So the idea would be to have Dr. Wong go to the caves, and then take a bunch of pictures, and send them back to us with his iPhone?"

"Exactly. But to go there, he needs a reason for doing so and that reason should come from somebody in the Beijing government, say a physician who's following the Coronavirus epidemic. And the names of those people are published in a local medical journal."

"Yes, I see where you're going with this. We task our tech guy, Jason Hardy, to forge an official document that gives Dr. Wong permission to visit the caves, say he's on some kind of research project. And he addresses that document to Dr. Yang. When Yang sees the document he won't be able to refuse our man permission to enter the caves because it comes from Beijing."

* * *

The ruse worked to perfection but it required three weeks of patience and persistence. And the take was better than expected: eleven sharp-as-a-razor photographs of the production process inside Cave No. One and a group of pictures showing the small cigarette packages coming of a moving belt in Cave No. 2. Another photo pictured a man wearing a black-on-white badge with the words 'Inspector' engraved on the badge, along with his name—Ying Fu Wang.

Next step: forward the 'take' to CIA headquarters.

# SIXTEEN

*In the office of Far East Division chief Walter Jensen. Jensen is speaking to his deputy, John Grove.*

"Looks like we've finally rounded the circle, John. This package from our guys in Beijing pretty much seals the deal."

"What now, Walt?"

"I'm going to forward this material directly to the White House. The president wants his National Security Advisor, General David Fisher, to handle whatever fallout we get from Beijing. He'll likely want to confront the Chinese ambassador—again—with this new evidence.

* * *

There were no witnesses, but David Fisher, in his report to the president, wrote that the Chinese ambassador emphatically denied what he saw spread out on the table. He claimed the CIA had fabricated the whole thing, just to embarrass the Chinese government at its leader Xi Jinping.

Fisher insisted that the ambassador report the confrontation to his superiors in Beijing, which he did.

Forty-eight hours later, the ambassador told Fisher that Beijing was adamant: a scenario designed by the CIA's psych warfare staff, consisting of lies and fabricated evidence. Fisher responded that, in his opinion, the Chinese had made a huge mistake, one that would almost certainly be regarded by the average Chinese citizen as an affront to world order and stability.

* * *

Three days later, the White House released the photographs and accompanying texts to the country's four major television networks and the wire services of every news outlet in the United States and Europe, also the same material with Chinese voice-overs and Mandarin-language texts.

Within hours Beijing's walled government compound was surrounded by Chinese citizens, many of them carrying placards demanding the resignation of Chairman Xi, accusing his government of allowing China's reputation to be sullied by self-serving government bureaucrats. Several of the protestors attempted to throw Molotov cocktail fire-bombs over the walls.

That same day, four of China's ambassadors were recalled to Beijing; those serving in Washington, London, Paris and Moscow.

President Oglethorpe texted a congratulatory message to CIA Director David Perkins, asking him to forward his message to those members of the agency's psych warfare staff, also to the agency's team in Beijing.

The good news: An Associated Press reporter in Beijing noted that Chinese military police had subdued the near-riot in Tiananmen Square and that life in China, at least in the capital, was slowly returning to normal.

# SEVENTEEN

At San Francisco's International Airport, Chang Chi Lee made his way through the immigration and customs checkpoints without any trouble, his visitor's visa telling the immigration officer that he had an invitation from St. Mary's Mercy hospital in Chinatown and would be working with its staff, doing research on the novel Coronavirus.

He asked the immigration official to take his word for it, assuming the man couldn't read Mandarin Chinese. If he could it would have identified Lee as a licensed epidemiologist, with a doctor's degree from Beijing University's School of Medicine.

He collected his luggage from the arrivals terminal baggage carousel, made his way to one of the airport's taxi stands and, thirty minutes later, stepped into the hospital's entrance. Zhang Wei was there to meet him.

* * *

"You are Chang Chi Lee?"

"That's right, and I assume you are Zhang Wei Ying?"

"Yes, yes, please come in. We've been expecting you. There's an apartment building across the street from the hospital and we've reserved one of their units for you, for as long as you wish."

"That's most generous of you, Zhang Wei. And I can't thank you enough for your invitation."

"How was your flight?"

"Uneventful but certainly different. There were only five of us passengers. Each of us was required to wear a mask, as did the flight attendants, we were required to sit at least ten feet apart and the two meals we were served were wrapped in what they claimed to be a virus-resistant plastic envelope. So, yes, everyone seems to be taking this pandemic quite seriously."

\* \* \*

The two men moved to the hospital's library, Zhang Wei put out the Do Not Disturb sign and the two men talked for about an hour.

Highlights:

\* \* \*

Dr. Lee was born in Wuhan and his elderly father still lives there. They use Skype and Face Book to stay in touch. In late December 2019, both of them became infected with the Coronavirus, probably because they were living in the same apartment building, about one kilometer from the animal market where the virus is thought to have originated. Dr. Lee insisted that both he and his father remain inside the building for at least fourteen days, preparing their own meals and refusing to accept visitors. Although he didn't realize it at the time, this self-quarantine allowed him and his father gradually to recover and at the end of the third week both father and son were well enough to leave their quarters and move freely about the city.

The only possible conclusion: both he and his father had become immune to the Coronavirus. This, despite the fact that the Wuhan authorities—after receiving daily reports from five hospitals and two morgues—announced that 1,736 residents had died.

When asked about his United States entry visa, Dr. Lee said it is unrestricted, meaning he can stay for up to one year. But, if the two men's collaborative research appears to be gaining ground, he'll apply for a Green Card and eventual U.S. Citizenship.

And, yes, he read the *Wall Street Journal* article about Zhang Wei's discovery of the immunity-inducing protein. That kind of news—because of its significance—would reach Chinese readers within seconds. He said that to try finding a method by which to synthesize that protein, to produce a vaccine, would be any physician's highest calling. And, he added, he was here to help do just that.

What about his father? Does he know about this?

He does, via Face Time twelve hours ago. And he wants to be part of the program. His father knows of a group of doctors in Wuhan who are doing the same kind of research, to find a vaccine that will be available and plentiful. He said the Chinese are well aware that the leaders of many countries blame the Chinese government for failing to control the spread of the virus and that is a powerful incentive, that they be the first to find an effective vaccine.

Then the two physicians talked about a partnership, which, if structured correctly, could include the father's participation. Zhang Wei was quick to add that the fledgling corporation— Covid Control—was already capitalized at nearly $2,000,000 with shareholders checking the Nasdaq listings every morning. Thus, funding their research would not be a problem, so long as they issued weekly progress reports to satisfy their investors.

As with any corporation, they needed a board of directors and they quickly identified four physicians, each one on the staff of St. Mary's Mercy Hospital. For expertise, they recruited a specialist from the nearby office of Jensen and Jensen, the nation's leading producer of pharmaceutical products. Dr. William David Huang was a third-generation Chinese-American immunologist, with twenty-six years of experience. It would be Dr. Huang's task to design and then supervise the equipping of the laboratory in which the synthesizing process would take place.

* * *

Ten days later this article appeared on Page One of *The San Francisco Chronicle.*

## CHINESE MEDDLING, AGAIN?

By Franklin Mackenzie, staff reporter

We have learned that San Francisco's FBI office has been tasked to determine what, if any, pressure has been applied on the newly-minted corporation, Covid Control, by undercover agents of Beijing's intelligence service.

Covid Control is a recently incorporated start-up laboratory that is attempting to develop a vaccine which, if successful, would give its users immunity to the novel Coronavirus.

The company's board chairman is Dr. Zhang Wei Ying, one of the senior physicians at St. Mary's Mercy hospital in Chinatown. Dr. Ying has a long history of dealing with Covid-19, the often-fatal disease caused by the Coronavirus.

According to our source in the FBI's San Francisco Field Office, PRC intelligence officers Heng Bo Hui and Ye Ru Yong, working undercover in China's San Francisco Consulate, have threatened Dr.

Ying. They have told him that it is up to the *Chinese* to develop an anti-Coronavirus vaccine, because that is where the problem began. The Chinese leaders in Beijing, they claim, insist that the Americans have no right to interfere. The problem originated in China and it is up China to solve it.

When confronted with this threat, Dr. Ying responded that any such delay could easily result in the deaths of thousands more Chinese, as well a many, many others. His words, he said, fell on deaf ears.

Covid Control will continue its work, the Chinese know this and they are not happy.

# EPILOGUE

Heng Bo Hui's report to Beijing notwithstanding, the Chinese—at last report—were still attempting to develop a vaccine, the work concentrated, ironically, in a Wuhan laboratory located not ten kilometers from where the worldwide pandemic began. Many of those outside China, also experts in the field, doubt they can do it.

Meanwhile, Covid Control continues its work and is making significant progress. More than 300 Bay Area volunteers have been tested and in every case the immunotherapy has been successful. While not yet the panacea solution that everyone is hoping for, prospects are indeed encouraging.

Stay tuned.

# ABOUT THE AUTHOR

John Sager is a retired United States intelligence officer whose services for the CIA, in various capacities, spanned more than a half-century. A widower, he makes his home in the Covenant Shores retirement community on Mercer Island, Washington.

©Yuen Lui Studio, 2003

Printed in the United States
By Bookmasters